KIPLING

STORYTELLER OF EAST AND WEST

Books by Gloria Kamen

Fiorello
Charlie Chaplin
Kipling

KIPLING

STORYTELLER
OF EAST AND WEST

by GLORIA KAMEN

ATHENEUM   1985   NEW YORK

Library of Congress Cataloging in Publication Data

Kamen, Gloria.
Kipling: storyteller of East and West.

SUMMARY: A brief biography of the teller of tales
about East and West, from his early years in India
and schooling in England to his later success as
reporter, poet, and short story writer.
1. Kipling, Rudyard, 1865-1936—Biography—Juvenile
literature.   2. Authors, English—19th century—Biography
—Juvenile literature.   (1. Kipling, Rudyard, 1865-1936.
2. Authors, English)   I. Title.
PR4856.K35   1985   828'.809   (B) (92)   85-7945
ISBN 0-689-31195-8

Text and pictures copyright © 1985 by Gloria Kamen
All rights reserved
Published simultaneously in Canada by
Collier Macmillan Canada, Inc.
Text set by Linoprint Composition, Inc., New York City
Printed and bound by Maple-Vail Book Manufacturing Group,
Binghamton, New York
First Edition

ACKNOWLEDGMENTS

The author wishes to acknowledge with thanks the kind assistance given by Professor Vasant Parab, dean of the JJ School of Art in Bombay, India, to Mr. George Lindsay of the Brattleboro Public Library and to Mr. Louis Jacob of the Library of Congress, Asian division, for providing valuable information for this book. Thanks also to Mr. R. C. Taylor and the knowledgable guides at Bateman's and to Dr. and Mrs. Slater for taking me there.

For sparking the idea, my thanks to Peggy Thomson and other members of our writer's group, especially Gene Namovicz, whose suggestions were most helpful. To Marcia Marshall, I am indebted, for the third time, for her enthusiastic support.

To Elliot

CONTENTS

Kipling's Books for Children

The Jungle Books   1894
The Second Jungle Book   1895
Captains Courageous   1897
Stalky & Co.   1899
Kim   1901
Just So Stories   1902
Puck of Pooks Hill   1906
Rewards and Fairies   1910

INTRODUCTION

INDIA, a land alive with color, mystery and legends was Rudyard Kipling's home for the first five years of his life. Less than ten years before his British parents arrived in Bombay, India, there had been a war. The Queen of England had sent troops to help the Indians establish order and later claimed the vast country (more than ten times larger than her own) as her colony.

India seemed a strange and sometimes frightening country to the British families who went there. But some, like Rudyard's parents, learned to love it and lived there most of their lives.

Europeans were called "sahibs" in the 1900s by their Indian servants. Rudyard was a "little sahib" to Meeta and his nursemaid. Our story will tell how he grew to be one of the best writers about the East, the author of the *Just So Stories, The Jungle Books,* and of many others you may have heard or read. It begins when Rudyard was a small boy in the city of Bombay, India.

A Little Sahib

RUDDY was already awake when Ayah came into the room. The cooling breeze that always came with the dawn woke him. Outside, jewel-bright colors of a Bombay morning tinted the fine netting surrounding his bed. A hot pink sky was turning turquoise, with the harbor water already a dark purple.

Today, Ayah, as Ruddy called his Portugese nurse-maid, was taking him to the open market to buy fruits and vegetables for the household. Though the market was some distance away, he was now old enough to walk alongside his sister's carriage while they shopped.

After a quick breakfast, Ruddy and Ayah walked toward the open market with baby Trix nestled inside the white wicker carriage. The clatter of shoppers and high-pitched calls of vendors could be heard a long way off. Holding tightly to the carriage handle, Ruddy inched his way along the stalls. On shelves above his head stood stacks of baskets and brass plates. Pyramids of fragrant flat breads were being sold by a turbaned, brown-skinned vendor. An old woman, draped in layers of faded cotton, sat cross-legged behind piles of pomegranates and ripe coconuts. Ruddy recognized the smell of curry that escaped from a steaming pot nearby. A heavy basket brushed his shoulder and an old man's bony elbow sent him stumbling over a pile of ripe bananas.

"If I had my pony here I'd ride him up and down and shout, OUT OF MY WAY, OUT OF MY WAY, Ruddy is coming!" he told Ayah.

Suddenly, he felt himself lifted in Ayah's strong arms. A lumbering old bull was slowly making its way between the food stalls, here and there nibbling some green vegetable. Everyone moved aside. No one seemed frightened. It was, Ayah said, a sacred animal and could go wherever it pleased. She sniffed as she said this, for Ayah was a Christian and did not believe in sacred animals.

But Ruddy knew that Meeta did. Meeta, his Hindu servant, often took Ruddy to the temple where he prayed. There the boy saw jeweled elephants carved in stone, painted statues of bulls and, most puzzling, statues of gods with four, five and six arms.

Meeta did not believe in killing *any* animals, not even a rat, he told Ruddy. Nor would he eat meat. Cows and bulls were protected by the gods and therefore sacred, he had said.

There were other times when Meeta told "the little sahib," as he called Ruddy, stories of tigers that haunted villages, of a giant turtle that was said to support a mountain on his back. He talked about the mysterious legends of India in Hindi, for Meeta was not good at speaking English. Ruddy, who spent most of his time with servants, understood the Indian language well. In fact, it was Ayah who reminded him each evening to speak English, not Hindi, to his parents as he was gently pushed through the dining room door after dinner.

ON THE WAY BACK from the market Ayah stopped in front of a roadside shrine. Ruddy watched her bend down to pray before the figure of a Catholic saint. This was not one of Meeta's gods. But Ayah had told him there was really only one God. He was confused. His parents never spoke to him of God or gods.

Though his parents were not rich by English standards, they had a cook, gardeners, and nursemaids for their children, for servants cost very little in India. There were dogs, ponies, horses and carts for Ruddy to play with, but few playmates other than his younger sister. Ruddy spent short periods each day with his mother, even less time after Trix was born. His mother had been ill. The heat, the different food, and most of all, the sudden fevers, were unlike anything she had known

5

in England. She had come to India only seven years ago as a young bride, just before Ruddy was born.

Mrs. Kipling was troubled by the halting way her son spoke English. Her husband, Lockwood, assured her that this would change once Ruddy attended school. Lockwood was a sculptor who came to Bombay to teach sculpture and pottery in the JJ Art School. Across the garden of their large house was his studio filled with colorful paint, clay and modeling tools. Watching his father's quick fingers form the head of an animal from wet clay delighted and amazed young Ruddy. Sometimes he tried pinching and squeezing clay, but his animal looked very different from his father's. "In time," his father told him, "you will learn how."

But there was little time for his father to teach him, for unknown to Ruddy, his parents were already planning to send him to school in England...six thousand miles away.

Parting

THERE WERE days when Ruddy's mother watched him with a mixture of worry and sadness. It was not like her. She was usually happy to be with him, often sitting at the piano to sing to him her favorite Welsh songs. She wanted to talk about his going away, to tell him it was necessary...to tell him it was the only way he could receive a traditional British education. But it was too painful to talk about. His mother believed that he was too young to fully understand.

Ruddy noticed that when he walked with his mother along the river to watch the Arab dhows rocking gently along the shore, her eyes wandered toward The Towers of Silence nearby. Huge birds with ugly heads and wings like the frayed capes of witches flapped around the tower. The vultures, scavengers of decaying dead meat, filled her with disgust. They were reminders of the fever and cholera that came with the rainy season. Every year many children died of them. Alice Kipling had lost her third child shortly after it was born. So far, Trix, nearly three, and Ruddy, almost six, had been lucky...but for how long? There were no miracle drugs then, nor for that matter, any medical care Alice would trust in India. The water, the climate, even the servants were carriers of disease.

Painful as it was going to be, she would have to send her children away to a healthier, safer place. Almost all the English families in India made the same choice when their children were ready to begin school.

Trix was much too young to start school, too young to be sent away, and yet it would be cruel to separate Ruddy and Trix, for the two children had played together since she was born. Because of Trix's age, their mother could not think of where to send them. To her sisters? They had young children of their own. To ask them to care for two more, not just for a brief visit but for years, was unreasonable. As for Trix and Ruddy, their English relatives were complete strangers to them. It would not make the separation from their parents any easier. Besides, she realized Ruddy had been spoiled by the kind servants and could be demanding and willful.

After many hours of discussion, the Kiplings decided to board the children with a kindly English family for the first few years. When they were old enough they would be sent to boarding school.

Could anyone offering to care for two young children be anything but kind? The Kiplings didn't think so. So, without checking, they agreed to send Ruddy and Trix to Captain and Mrs. Holloway in Swansea, England, for a few years. They had heard of the Holloways from an advertisement in an English language newspaper in Bombay.

When the letter arrived from Captain and Mrs. Holloway agreeing to care for Master Rudyard and his sister, Ruddy had not yet learned how to recite the English alphabet. But in his head were the sounds, the words, the images of Meeta's India.

The family made preparations for the long journey to England, that far-off country Ruddy's parents called their home.

Salt Is the Flavor of Tears

MEETA and Ayah were there to say good-bye as the horse-drawn carriage came to take the Kiplings to the harbor. Ruddy didn't understand why the servants were being left behind.

"Come back and be a burra sahib," said Meeta when he said good-bye.

"Come back, baba," said Ayah daubing her eyes.

"Yes, I will come back and I'll be a burra sahib bahadur," Ruddy answered in Hindi.

Down at the harbor Arab dhows and tiny Indian rafts were dwarfed by the ocean-going steamship waiting to carry them to England. Ruddy was looking forward to the long ocean voyage, especially as both Momma and Poppa were going along. Lockwood had not been back to England since he left over seven years ago, and Alice had gone only once when Ruddy was two to await the birth of her second child. Ruddy, whose real name was Rudyard, was told he was named for the lake in Wales where his parents first met. Even in England, Rudyard was an unusual name for a boy, but his mother preferred it to his other name, John.

It was June when they left the west coast of India to cross the Arabian Sea, the Red Sea, and the Mediterranean...and cold bleak December by the time they arrived in Portsmouth, England. Never before had Trix or Rudyard spent so much of their day with Momma and Poppa. Every evening their mother read to them and sang songs. It was a long, happy voyage — happy that is, for the children.

"Please Ruddy," his mother said after Trix fell asleep, "don't let Trix forget me. She is so young."

This puzzled her young son. Why, he wondered, did he need to remind Trix when she saw Mother every day? But Ruddy asked each morning and Trix, just turned three, answered she "bemembered Momma."

The excitement of the trip left little time for solving the mystery. So far as he knew they were going for a visit to Momma's and Poppa's family. And when it was over they would all travel back together to Bombay.

DURING the long journey, whether out of fear of Rudyard's temper or to delay the grief of parting, Alice and Lockwood never explained the reason for the trip.

After the ship arrived in England on a typical gray winter morning, they left Portsmouth harbor for the town of Southsea. There, at the house called Lorne Lodge, Captain and Mrs. Holloway welcomed the four Kiplings. The ugly stone house bore no resemblance to the large white house and pleasant garden Ruddy had left in Bombay. In the doorway stood a woman in black, a frozen smile on her face. Her twelve-year-old son peered from behind his mother. Rudyard took an immediate dislike to both of them.

For six days his mother and father stayed at Lorne Lodge, telling Ruddy that Mr. and Mrs. Holloway were to be called Uncle Harry and Aunty Rosa, that the Holloways were very pleased to have him stay.

Rudyard was tired of the visit and wanted to leave. He did not like his new aunty. She was nothing like the gentle ayah in Bombay. Neither did she call him "sahib."

For six days his mother wept from time to time but said nothing. Even then his parents did not try to explain that they were returning to India without him. On the seventh day, at dawn, Alice and Lockwood kissed their sleepy children...and left.

THE MISERY of that morning remained in Rudyard's memory for many years. When he wrote the story, *Baa, Baa, Black Sheep*, he described it in this way. (The boy in

the story, named Punch, is himself and Judy is his sister, Trix.)

When the tears ceased the house was very still. Aunty Rosa had decided that it was better to let the children "have their cry out." Punch raised his head from the floor and sniffed mournfully. Judy was nearly asleep...There was a distant, dull boom in the air...a repeated heavy thud. Punch knew that sound in Bombay in the monsoon. It was the sea — the sea that must be crossed before anyone could get to Bombay.

"Quick, Ju!" he cried. "We're close to the sea. I can hear it! Listen! That's where they've went. P'raps we can catch them if we was in time. They didn't mean to go without us. They've only forgot!"

...He took Judy by the hand and the two ran hatless in the direction of the sound of the sea.

Salt is the flavor of tears... It was left to Aunty Rosa to tell the children that *she* was totally and fully in charge from that day on, that their parents *were not coming back.*

Fat Cats & Griffins

GRIM ROSA HOLLOWAY believed she had two important missions: to teach Rudyard about God and to teach him to read. She read to the children regularly from the Bible. But her telling of the Creation of the World was very different from Meeta's. It was puzzling to the six-year-old boy who had not heard it before and who was forbidden to ask questions.

The story of the Creation in the Bible filled Ruddy with wonder, delight and some confusion. Left to find his own answers, he mixed part of India's legends with the story from the Bible. When Aunty Rosa overheard him tell his imaginative blend of East and West in a story to Trix, she was furious. "God," she told him, "heard every word" and was *very angry.*

It seemed, after a while, that everything Ruddy did or said made either God or Aunty Rosa *very angry.* Little boys, he was told over and over again, were not expected to speak unless spoken to, were not to sit on sofas, or to ask too many questions.

After five years of being treated like a little prince by the numerous servants in Bombay, his new life in Lorne Lodge seemed unbearable. His longing to discover, to explore, to understand were called "showing off." Mrs. Holloway saw Rudyard as a willful, troublesome boy.

Adding to his unhappiness was Mrs. Holloway's son who found new ways each day to torment him. At bedtime, he forced sleepy, tired Ruddy, to tell him what he had done that day. By means of cross-examining him, he managed to get Ruddy to keep changing his answers. Each time Ruddy hoped he would find the one that would allow him, finally, to go to bed. The next morning his confused answers were reported to Aunty Rosa as, "Ruddy tells lies." Punishment followed. With the firm belief that "to spare the rod is to spoil the child," Mrs. Holloway beat him with a cane.

In the bleak house in Southsea only Captain Holloway showed Rudyard any kindness. But the Captain was ill and died two years after Ruddy came to stay, and then there was no one to offer a kind word, except little Trix...and they were not together most of the day. More and more Rudyard withdrew into the world of his imagination. During the long hours he spent locked inside a damp, cold playroom to play with nothing but a few broken toys, he created his own games. There were no

Rudyard,
age six

books in the playroom. In any case, Ruddy could barely read after a year of lessons. Aunty Rosa was convinced that he was not only willful but stupid as well.

Her method of teaching the children to read was done in the same harsh manner as her lessons on the Bible. It was unsuccessful. When the reading lessons first began, Mrs. Holloway sat Rudyard on a table and told him that A B meant ab. "Why?" asked Rudyard innocently. "*Because I tell you it does*...and you've got to say it," was her answer. Even Trix, who was learning to read at the same time, was doing better than her older brother. She could read "*a fat cat sat on a mat*" while Rudyard was still spelling it out, letter by letter. Left alone with Trix after one of their lessons, Ruddy said, "You're too little to understand, Trix...you haven't the brains to know the *hard* things about reading. *I* want to know why *T* with *hat* after it should be *that*." Four-year-old Trix only looked puzzled. And there was no one else around to answer his question.

After dreary months of struggle with sentences like "the *Cat* lay on the *Mat* and the *Rat* came in," there came a day that was nothing short of magical. In a dark corner of an unused cupboard, Rudyard found an old magazine for children. Inside its covers were poems, folk tales and exciting pictures. There were knights in armor, wolves and an imaginary animal called the griffin. It seemed to be flying over a group of terrified shepherds. The words under the pictures were much too difficult for Rudyard to read...but he desperately wanted to know what they meant. Following the black letters on the page with his finger, his mouth formed sounds that suddenly became words; the words began to form sentences, and to his delight he discovered he was reading! But the picture of the griffin still puzzled him.

The next evening, still flushed with excitement over his new discovery, he asked Aunty Rosa what the word "griffin" meant. Since griffins were not in the Bible or in his schoolbooks, Aunty Rosa sent him to bed without answering.

Books arrived along with letters from his parents after they were told that Ruddy could read. Though Mrs. Holloway often disapproved of the kind of books he was sent, she did not feel she could keep Ruddy from reading them. One of his favorites was *Robinson Crusoe.* His newfound pleasure in reading, however, gave Aunty Rosa another way to punish Rudyard. He was forbidden to read anything but his lesson books or the Bible without her permission. But Ruddy managed to read and reread his favorite books by hiding them under his jacket before being locked in the playroom. Sometimes the strain of reading in the dimly lit basement made the words dance and blur before his eyes.

UNLIKE her behavior toward Rudyard, Mrs. Holloway treated Trix with a great deal more kindness. Pretty, gentle Trix gave her no trouble. Aunty Rosa kept Trix away from her brother as much as possible, telling her that Ruddy was bad.

"Why are you always so bad?" Trix asked one day when they were alone. Ruddy only shook his head and said he honestly didn't know. The children at school were unfriendly and bullied him. The devil boy, as he called Rosa's son, saw to that. Only she, Trix, he said, gave him any love or kindness.

Ruddy's weekly letters to his parents were written under the watchful eyes of Aunty Rosa. Letters from India came in return, but there was no mention of when they would all be together again. As the years passed, India and the parents he loved became a vague memory. The "real world" was now his prison house from which he escaped only at Christmas time.

Wombats, Pugdogs and Painters

NEITHER AUNT GEORGIE, his mother's sister whom he visited each Christmas, nor his parents knew anything about his unhappiness at Lorne Lodge.

Aunt Georgie was married to a well-known painter, Edward Burne-Jones. Their large house in Fulham was filled with finished and unfinished paintings of mythical and historic subjects. Charcoal sketches and plaster casts of famous statues were scattered about the studio. Whiffs of linseed oil and turpentine drifted from the bright airy room where Uncle Ned worked. It reminded Rudyard of his father's studio in Bombay. His other uncle, Edward Poynter, who was also a painter, would often visit Fulham at Christmas as well.

There were few rules at Aunt Georgie's house. Ruddy and his cousins were free to wander about as they pleased.

To the delight of all of them, big and little, Uncle Ned would sometimes pick up his pen or a piece of chalk and start to draw. Pictures of wombats (a kind of opossum), pigs and pugdogs seem to jump off the page. As he sketched, he made up animal adventures to go with the drawings. Not only did everyone applaud his silly stories but each of them was encouraged to make up his own. Ruddy understood for the first time that art and storytelling gave pleasure not only to the listener but to the creator as well. It was his uncle's love of fantasy, of the unusual that excited his young mind.

The house in Fulham was the place Rudyard first heard *The Arabian Nights,* read aloud by Aunt Georgie. Like the Arabian Nights, Christmas was enchantment. And when it ended, he was like the prince turned back into a frog.

The holiday never lasted long enough. In a few weeks he would be the black sheep of Lorne Lodge once again. And everything he wanted and so desperately needed: love, fun, companionship, was taken away from him.

Each Christmas, all that Aunt Georgie and Uncle Ned saw when Rudyard arrived was a well-fed, excited boy. He gave no hint to anyone of his miserable life in the stone house at Southsea.

But it was during his fifth visit that his cousins,

Philip and Jenny, noticed something was wrong, that Ruddy was crying in his sleep and bumping into things during the day. When asked what was wrong, Rudyard would not explain. It was embarrassing for an eleven-year-old boy to be caught crying. How could he tell them that the saddest time of his life was when he had to return to Lorne Lodge?

"CHILDREN tell little more than animals," said Rudyard many years later. "They accept what comes to them as the way things are." And then he added: "Badly treated children have a clear idea of what they are likely to get if they betray the secret of the prison house."

But fear was the thing that revealed his secret to his family. That winter, word came back to Aunt Georgie from Lorne Lodge that something was wrong with Ruddy. He was acting peculiar. He saw shapes and shadows that weren't there. His grades in school were worse than ever, and he complained that he couldn't read his schoolbooks. "Lazy, careless, just the usual excuses," complained Mrs. Holloway.

Rudyard was confused and upset. His mind seemed to be playing tricks...and worry turned into uncontrollable fear.

What he did not know was that he was half blind!

What Is Gone Is Gone, Gone

A DOCTOR sent by his aunt and uncle made the startling discovery. He noticed the boy's near blindness when Ruddy entered the dim parlor and knocked over the entire tea tray. He hadn't seen it, he said. Further examination proved he was telling the truth.

The letter sent to his parents about Ruddy's blindness was received with shock and disbelief. Mrs. Kipling arranged to leave India at once. But "at once" meant months of travel before she would arrive in England. Perhaps for this reason she did not write to say she would be coming. Instead, she appeared one chilly day in March, five years after the dawn when she had kissed her children good-bye.

Out of a four-wheeled cab stepped a lovely lady who greeted the children with a hug. It was their mother, they were told. But for his poor eyesight, Ruddy might have recognized her. Still, she seemed a stranger to them. Trix barely remembered her, just as her mother had feared.

It was in the evening soon after their mother arrived that she fully realized the harsh treatment her son had endured. When she bent down to kiss him goodnight, Ruddy automatically threw up his arm. He had come to expect blows, not kisses, at bedtime and had put up his arm to protect himself.

"WHAT IS GONE is gone, gone." So goes an old Hindu proverb. Gone was half of Ruddy's eyesight. Gone was five years of childhood. Gone too, was his mother's unquestioned belief in decency and kindness.

She took her children away from Lorne Lodge to a farmhouse on the edge of Epping Forest. Trix and Ruddy were free to roam and explore the fields and forests, to read, or to do nothing. It was like a nine-month, wonderful Christmas holiday!

Fitted with a pair of steel-rimmed glasses, Ruddy was able to read again…and no rules were set by his mother on what and when he could read. No longer did he face the "devil boy" each night, or the bullies in the school playground by day. His mother was gentle and loving and spent the months of their holiday trying to know her son and daughter better. In turn they were finding out more about her.

By the end of the stay Rudyard discovered that his mother wrote poetry and that his father also liked to write. Alice told her son that books and pictures were among the most important things in the world to them.

This was *his* family just as he hoped it would be!

FROM THE FARM Alice took her children to a small house in London for the remainder of her stay. It was painful for her to tell them that she would soon need to return to India. So long as their father stayed in India, where there were no adequate schools for them, Trix and Rudyard needed to remain in England without her. Her place, she felt, was with her husband.

Trix, just turned eight, would not be ready for boarding school for two more years. With much hesitation, Mrs. Kipling sent her daughter back to Lorne Lodge, where pretty, gentle Trix had always been well-treated.

Still to be settled before she left was the problem of her son's further education. Rudyard had done poorly at school. Some schools would be closed to him because of his grades. Some schools were more expensive than Rudyard's father could afford on his modest salary. There was also the question of Ruddy's poor eyesight. In the end, Mrs. Kipling decided to send him to Westward Ho, a boys' boarding school in Devonshire whose headmaster was their friend, Cromwell Price.

It was an odd choice in some ways. Most of the boys in the school were sons of military men who planned to make a career of the army, navy, or civil service. Physical fitness was important at Westward Ho. Soccer, rugger (similar to football), and cricket were all part of the daily routine. For Rudyard, who could barely see beyond the edge of his arm, taking part in field games was nearly impossible. Mrs. Kipling counted on Cromwell Price to solve this problem for him.

Rudyard, just three weeks past his twelfth birthday, pudgy, short for his age, wearing thick glasses (the *only* boy in the school who did), enrolled in Westward Ho. "Gigger" became his nickname. It was short for gig-lamps, the word used by his classmates for eyeglasses. With a hint of a mustache above his upper lip, his slightly olive complexion, he made a striking appearance. Though he was the youngest boy in his grade, he looked like one of the oldest.

The school was only a few years old, inexpensive, with fairly primitive facilities. The meals, Rudyard wrote home, would cause a prison riot. At times, Kipling and his friends were so hungry they traded their few possessions to buy extra food.

Not good at sports and only average in his studies, it was the headmaster, affectionately called Uncle Crom, who discovered Ruddy's special talent: writing. So, while

A is a pair of bellows
B. India rubber tubing
C.- A penny whistle

Of course you can see
that the power of noise
is almost unlimited
and as it can inconveni[ence]
your neighbor with very
little caution we "laid on"
that instrument to a neat
[...] your study like th[...]

The Headmaster

other boys were out on the soccer field, Rudyard was allowed the full use of Uncle Crom's well-stocked library, to read anything he pleased. Rudyard began to read poetry, essays, novels, far in advance of books boys his age would usually read. He soon started writing his own poetry, slipping copies into his letters to his parents.

Schoolboy "Gigger" was not all owlish. At times he was like the noisy bluejay and as mischevious as a young raccoon. Along with two friends as free-spirited as himself, he liked to play practical jokes on teachers and classmates alike. He happily and frequently broke the rules. His friend, nicknamed Stalky, was their leader, with McTurk, and himself, Ruddy, as accomplices.

In words and drawings, Rudyard told in detail how the terrible three rigged up an "infernal machine" in their dormitory. With a penny whistle, a piece of rubber tubing, and a pair of bellows, bought or stolen from somewhere, they sent whistling noises into the adjoining study. By placing the tube into a hole in the ceiling and pumping the bellows with their foot, they kept the sound going for two hours without anyone figuring out where it was coming from. Another plan to hide a dead and very smelly cat in the rafters of the next dormitory was never carried out. How it might have turned out was told in one of Kipling's stories about his school days in the book, *Stalky & Co.*

By his third year at school, taller, older, already smoking a pipe, Rudyard looked the upperclassman he was. Uncle Crom appointed him editor of the school paper, a good preparation, he discovered later, for what was to follow. Unlike his friends at school, he had no clear idea of what he would do after graduation. Actually, his parents settled that for him.

Without any word to their son, Mr. and Mrs. Kipling had collected the poems Rudyard had written during his school days and had them printed in a little booklet. They passed the few copies around among their friends in Lahore where they were now living. Some of the writing was good enough to impress the editor of a small English-language newspaper in that city. The editor, Mr. Wheeler, offered to put Rudyard on his newspaper staff.

"Come to Lahore," said a letter from his parents at graduation, "we have found you a job."

Just short of his seventeenth birthday, Rudyard booked passage for his return to India. He was going home.

It had been over ten years since the little boy promised to return a "burra sahib."

Tales from the Hills

SO MUCH had happened in ten years. The fuzzy shadow on his upper lip was now a full-grown mustache. His pipe, his British suit and manners changed the awkward schoolboy into a British "sahib" looking older than his seventeen years. There was pride, not childish arrogance on his face...and pleasure. What would his father think of him? And what would he think of his father when they met?

Only once since he left India were they together. It was during the Paris Exposition of 1878, when his father went to Paris to set up the Indian Pavilion for the fair. Rudyard was thirteen then. They had had a wonderful time together. Would it be different now, living day to day as a family? He had heard stories from classmates who said after a visit to their family that their parents "were not the sort of people they cared for." In a few days he would find out. Rudyard's father and Mr. Wheeler, his employer, would be waiting for him when he arrived at the train station in Lahore.

As the ship docked at Bombay harbor, the sights and sounds of his childhood welcomed him. The vivid colors of India, so different from the ash grays and dull browns of London, delighted him. The throaty sounds of hawkers, the click, click of rickshaws, the babble of shoppers, children and their ayahs all seemed just as he had left them. He could smell the melted ghee, the flat breads baking in the ovens, the spices…all the same, the same. Only he had changed.

On the train from Bombay to Lahore the language of his childhood came back to him. It was as though a lock had sprung open. Rudyard found himself speaking Hindi, using words he hadn't spoken since he was six. He wasn't even sure what they *meant* before they came pouring from his lips. The Indians he met were delighted to find an Englishman who could speak in their language, for at that time, very few Indians had learned to speak English.

During the four-day train trip, there was time to think back over his years at Westward Ho and at Lorne Lodge. If there was someone to blame for his unhappy years at Southsea, it was not his parents. They had done only what seemed sensible at the time. It was Aunty Rosa and her devil boy he blamed and hated still. In dreams he saw himself set fire to their house and watched it burn to the ground.

Thanks to Cromwell Price and his happier years at Westward Ho, he had become more confident and secure again. His new job as a newspaper reporter would prove whether he had any writing talent.

When his train arrived in Lahore, Mr. Wheeler and Rudyard's father greeted him warmly. It was as though this part of his life was following the saying of an old Hindu proverb:

> A son should be treated as a prince for five years; as a slave for ten years; but from his sixteenth birthday, as a close friend.

And as a beloved son and friend, he was welcomed home. It didn't take long for Rudyard to decide that his parents *were* the sort of people he cared for!

The long years of waiting were over. Rudyard was back home, in India.

Lockwood Kipling was now a respected member of British Colonial society. Their Indian-style house with wide verandas and arched doorways had more than enough room to provide Rudyard with his own apartment and servants. As before, all his needs were attended to by them. His clothes were cleaned and set out for him, his food was prepared and served, and his horse and trap were made ready each day before he set off for work.

Trix was still in England finishing her last three years of schooling. When she returned, at age seventeen, the family was reunited for the first time in thirteen years. Their first Christmas together was a very happy one. But for many of their friends in India, with families divided, half in England, half in India, Christmas was a difficult, sad time. These words, part of a poem that Kipling wrote, describe their mood.

High noon behind the tamarisks — the sun
    is hot above us —
  As at Home the Christmas Day is
    breaking wan.
They will drink our healths at dinner —
    those who tell us how they love us,
  And forget us till another year be gone!

Until Trix became engaged and married, the four Kiplings enjoyed spending most of their time together, except during the monsoons, the rainy season of India. Each year around the middle of May, anyone who could leave the heat of Lahore traveled to the mountains. The town of Simla in the mountains near Tibet, where the Kiplings went, was free of the diseases that plagued the low lands.

Because of his work at the newspaper, Rudyard could not go with his family and remained, instead, in the big house with only his servant as company.

During the hottest summer nights, finding no relief anywhere inside the house, he moved his bed to the flat roof. Even there the pitiless heat made sleep impossible and Rudyard would dress and wander the streets until dawn. It was in the back alleys, the little shops and gambling dens where the life of the city went on in summer. This was the life and color he described in many of his newspaper stories for *The Civil and Military Gazette.*

Kipling's editor on the *Gazette* sent him to army barracks, princes' palaces, polo games, parades...any big or little event his readers would want to know about, for Rudyard was the only reporter on his paper. He was, in fact, fifty percent of the editorial staff as well. Mr. Wheeler depended on him to do half the writing for the *Gazette,* though Kipling was only seventeen at the time.

The *Gazette* was the only daily paper in the region. It came out every day whether or not the temperature in the office reached 110° with nothing but an overhead fan to stir the sizzling air around the room. It came out on days when Mr. Wheeler was ill and Rudyard wrote, edited, and proofread the entire paper. The workday sometimes stretched to ten, eleven and twelve hours.

Rudyard was highly amused when a letter came to the newspaper office complaining about something their reporter had written. He wrote back that as acting editor he'd investigate. But, he continued, the writer of the letter might find him biased since *he* was the reporter the person was complaining about.

From dawn to dark, six days a week, Rudyard labored over his writing. He not only had to fill in all the news but all the leftover space. So, when there wasn't enough news to fill the *Gazette,* he wrote stories. They were on every sort of subject. What they had in common was their setting: India.

Plain Tales From the Hills, as the forty stories he wrote were later called, were made into a set of small books that were sold in railway stations around India. When these three slim books were sent to London, their success changed his life.

The Jewel of India

AFTER SEVEN hard years as a newspaperman, Kipling was ready to leave India. At twenty-four he wanted to "explore new waters." He was going to London, England, to write, he told his editor.

The move he had made two years earlier to a larger newspaper in the bustling city of Allahabad had not turned out well. His new editor often criticized his work and considered Rudyard both overproud and overconfident. He warned Rudyard that the move to London might turn into a disaster. "Take it from me, you'll never be worth more than four hundred rupees a month to anyone," he said. Seven hundred rupees a month was Rudyard's pay at the time so it was quite clear that his boss didn't think much of his talent. Kipling took his last paycheck and left.

A long sea voyage and several months later, Kipling arrived in London, where he rented rooms above a shop called "Harris, the Sausage King." From his windows, he overlooked a noisy dance hall and a busy

London street. London was chills, fog and grit. There were no servants to prepare his food, no family to offer comfort. Rudyard was lonely. Why had he left India, he began to wonder? The reason, he knew, was to test his talent against the best writers of Britain…and he intended to succeed.

Day after day, he wrote stories, poems, more stories and more poems, sending them to newspapers and magazines. In less than a year, critics were talking about and praising the new, young writer from India. They were amazed that he was only twenty-four, for they believed from his writing that he was a much older man. His sudden success was compared to Charles Dickens, author of *Oliver Twist* and *Nicholas Nickleby.* When *Plain Tales From the Hills,* Kipling's first set of stories, appeared in London, they sold out.

Plain Tales From the Hills was published when the British were eager to find out more about India. British soldiers and civil servants were being sent to keep order in that vast country, for Britain had won India almost by accident. Now fathers, sons, husbands were living in that distant land, sometimes for years…some never returned. Since radio and television had not yet been invented, Englishmen knew little about life in that Asian country. Kipling's stories gave his readers a vivid picture of Anglo-Indian life.

LONDON of horse and buggy days, of sooty coal fires coming from thousands of smoky chimneys was described by Kipling in a short poem he sent back to India:

> The sky a greasy soup tureen,
>   Shuts down atop my brow.
> Yes, I have sighed for London Town
>   *And I have got it now.*

This unflattering view of London changed when Kipling made friends with other writers in that city. At a writer's club he frequently visited, he met an American, Wolcott Balestier, a publisher's agent eager to have Kipling's books sold in the United States. They became good friends.

Wolcott's older sister, Caroline, came from Vermont to visit her brother in London while Rudyard and Wolcott were writing a book together, *The Naulakha* (Jewel of India). It was a mystery that took place in both India and the United States. Kipling enjoyed the novelty of writing with someone else…and especially enjoyed his visits with the Balestiers. He spent more and more time with them. Caroline found her brother's friend charming and attractive, and it wasn't long before they were engaged to be married.

IN 1918, Kipling visited India for the last time. Bidding good-bye to friends, he started on the long sea journey to India for the third time in his life. He had not seen his parents in over a year and was eager to tell them of his plans to marry Caroline Balestier. Word of his amazing success as a writer had surely reached them in Lahore. He hoped his former editor had heard of it too!

A House Called Naulakha

THE VISIT to India was very brief. After announcing his plans to marry, Rudyard promised his parents they would soon meet his young bride, for he was taking Caroline on a trip around the world and would be coming with her to Lahore.

But the meeting didn't take place.

After returning to London, Rudyard and his new wife started their "round-the-world" tour by first visiting her family in Vermont, in the northeastern part of the United States. From there the journey to Japan was uneventful. In Yokohama, Japan, however, they heard shocking news. The bank to which their money had been sent in Yokohama failed, leaving them with no way to pay for the rest of their trip. All they had left was a return ticket and the little cash in their pockets, for Rudyard had used all his savings for the expensive journey.

What to do? The newlyweds decided to return to

the United States. They could live very cheaply, they agreed, on the Balestiers' farm in Vermont.

CAROLINE was already expecting her first child when they arrived in Vermont to stay with her brother, Beatty. After a few weeks they rented a tiny cottage nearby for ten dollars a month. Water for the cottage came from a single pipe connected to an outdoor spring and heat came from a second-hand stove. Kipling's workroom was no bigger than a closet. The views, however, were beautiful. The windows overlooked rolling hills and lush meadows.

The first Vermont winter was a picture perfect scene in dark green and dazzling white as far as the eye could see. Outside, the snowdrifts reached the level of the windowsills. Inside, baby Josephine, born that winter, slept peacefully under woolen blankets while Rudyard sat at his desk working on a magazine story about Indian forestry. The hiss of the stove, which kept the cottage snug and warm, sounded like the buzzing of a thousand insects on an Indian summer night.

A new idea, a story for children, suddenly took shape. Kipling began to imagine a brown-skinned boy sitting among wild animals...unafraid. Animals were his friends, for he had been raised by a she-wolf. Mowgli was the name given by Kipling to his imaginary "wild child."

While living in India Rudyard had heard many stories of children who had wandered into the jungle and were found years later, still alive. How they survived was a mystery. It was supposed that they followed the habits of animals, sleeping on the ground or in trees and eating raw food. One such child was discovered every few years in India. These stories go back even further, as far as Roman times, and the Roman myth of a she-wolf who nursed twin babies called Romulus and Remus.

Kipling's fictional boy, Mowgli, is not a true story. In the book, the boy speaks to animals in a language they understand. He talks to his friends, Baloo, the bear, Bagheera, the wise panther and to the Seeone wolf pack. Their adventures with the Banderlogs, Shere Khan, the cunning tiger, with monkeys and cobras make up many of the stories in *The Jungle Book*. Rikki-Tikki-Tavi's fight with a snake was based on a battle Kipling saw in a garden in Lahore between a mongoose and cobra.

Ideas for *The Jungle Book* came so swiftly that the stories almost wrote themselves, said Kipling. "After blocking out the main ideas in my head, the pen took charge and I watched it begin to write."

It was seven o'clock of a very warm evening in the Seeone hills when Father Wolf woke up from his day's rest, scratched himself, yawned, and spread out his paws one after the other to get rid of the sleepy feeling in their tips. Mother Wolf lay with her big grey nose dropped across her four tumbling, squealing cubs, and the moon shone into the mouth of the cave where they all lived.

So begins the story of Mowgli, the first book Kipling wrote for children. It was an immediate success. Mowgli's name became known to boys and girls world-wide. Although other authors imitated the Jungle Books, only one became equally popular: *The Story of Tarzan.*

Rudyard enjoyed the quiet of the Vermont country-side, which left him free to work undisturbed. Their neighbors in Brattleboro, mostly farmers, didn't know what to make of the famous English writer who lived among them. To the hard-working farmers, writing did not seem like honest labor. They couldn't see how Kipling could make as much as a hundred dollars out of a ten-cent bottle of ink and some pieces of paper. It amazed them that in only eighteen months he had gone from being a poor man to one of the richest in Brattle-boro. Money from his writing bought him four servants, a large new house, horses, a coachman and a fancy carriage. They were startled to see Caroline drive around town in a carriage driven by a scarlet-coated coachman wearing a top hat! Their new house, started soon after the snows melted that first winter, looked to his neighbors "like an ark set on a hill, as though a flood had cast it there." Kipling called it "his ship" and gave it the name "Naulakha." Money from the book written with Caroline's brother had helped pay for the house. Caroline Kipling made it clear that strangers were not welcomed at Naulakha, especially reporters.

"Mr. Kipling is the most unapproachable man in this country. He wishes to know and see nobody but Rudyard Kipling," said one of the newspapers. The townspeople also considered them unfriendly.

But there was misunderstanding on both sides, for Kipling said some very unkind things about the town only a few months after he arrived. "The talk on Main Street where every unimportant and tiny thing is reported, digested, discussed and rediscussed...a place," he said, "where people live lives disturbed by troubles and jealousies."

During their four years in Vermont, the Kiplings made few friends; they didn't see the need for more. Dave Cary, the baggage master at the Brattleboro railroad station, was one. "Kipling had the darndest mind," Mr. Cary told a reporter one day. "He wanted to know everything about everything, and never forgot what you told him. He would sit and listen and never stir."

Dr. Conland, another friend, agreed with Cary, for Kipling was always ready to listen to still another story of his adventures as a young fisherman on the Grand Banks. The sea and ships, ever a fascinating subject for his short stories, now became the background for Kipling's new book for children. Together with Dr. Conland, Kipling visited the Gloucester fishing fleets to gather information for *Captains Courageous*. In his first book about New England, Kipling tells the story of Harvey Cheyne, the spoiled son of a millionaire who is washed overboard into the frigid Atlantic. Harvey is rescued by the crew of a little fishing vessel and lives on board for many months. Through storms and disasters he learns that he, as well as every other man on ship, is responsible for their safe return to port.

Except for vacation trips, Kipling was content to remain in the pleasant countryside with his wife and daughters. The running of the household and farm he left to his wife. She took charge of the family accounts and sometimes hired her brother to help with the work around the farm, leaving her husband free to write.

A dispute over money broke out between Caroline and her brother, Beatty. They also quarreled over the use of a jointly-owned pasture, which she wished to turn into a formal garden. Her brother wanted it for his cows. Beatty was more heavily in debt each year as his brother-

Naulakha

in-law grew richer and richer. A fresh argument between the two ended with Beatty threatening to shoot Rudyard. Rudyard had Beatty arrested. The next day forty newspaper reporters arrived in Brattleboro. Everyone who had ever been denied an interview came to see Kipling squirm in the witness chair. The townspeople also crowded the small courtroom. Before the day ended, the Kiplings decided they could not remain in Vermont.

For almost four years Naulakha had been a happy home for the Kiplings. Another daughter, Elsie, was born there and her sister Josephine had thrived in the pleasant Vermont surroundings. But the battle with Beatty put an end to this peaceful life. Though they thought they would some day return, the Kiplings never did. Naulakha was sold, and even today sits like a deserted ship on Kipling Road.

Kim and the Lost Child

THAT SUMMER, the Kiplings left for England with their two small children. There was no longer any point to staying in Vermont where they had once enjoyed such privacy. Even though the charge against Beatty was dropped and the trial discontinued, Beatty would see to it that they would have neither privacy nor quiet if they returned.

AUNT GEORGIE and Uncle Ned, still the favorite aunt and uncle, offered the Kiplings their home when they arrived in England. Caroline was expecting another baby. Their son, John, was born soon after.

The five Kiplings moved into a rambling old farmhouse, The Elms, just across the green from the Burne-Joneses. Kipling's parents, who had retired after thirty years service in India, lived in Tisbury, not too far away. It was a special pleasure for Rudyard to be able to spend time with his parents again. He often visited them, and on many occasions, the three of them would talk about India.

Sitting comfortably across from his father in the study, his pipe sending spirals of smoke into the chilly air, Rudyard told his father he had been thinking about a story…about a boy in India. He wanted to write of a boy caught between the cultures of East and West, between the life of an Indian and the customs and ways of the British. *Kim* would be his name.

Together father and son talked about the idea, about the beggar boy who looked and sounded like a Hindu street urchin but had the truly Irish name of Kimball O'Hara. In the story, Kim meets an old Tibetan priest who is searching for a sacred river. Together they travel the roads of India. As the priest searches for his river, Kim discovers the secret of the emblem in the mystery locket around his neck. The discovery that his father was an Irish soldier, that he was not Indian, forces him to decide between living with his beloved priest or going into service for the British.

As the book unfolded, chapter by chapter, Rudyard and his father carefully polished each description, each vivid scene. When the book was finished, both father and son were pleased with the results.

THE CHILLY, drizzly winters in Britain were Kipling's least favorite time of year. He missed the warmth of India and the crisp cold of Vermont. So winter was the time for family vacations. Each year the Kiplings set off for a three-month visit to Cape Town, South Africa.

But in 1899, instead of leaving as usual for Cape Town, they planned a visit to the United States to visit Caroline's family. Her mother had not seen them in over two years and now Caroline had a new son to show her.

The Atlantic crossing was very cold and stormy, as unpleasant as any they could remember. The children were ill with whooping cough and Rudyard was hot with fever when they arrived in New York harbor. Rudyard was taken to a hospital seriously ill with a lung infection, and Josephine and Elsie were put in the care of a friend who lived nearby, on Long Island.

Josephine took a turn for the worse. All attempts to save her failed, and in February, she died. Only Caroline knew how deeply her husband would feel the death of his little daughter. It had been Josephine who repeated her father's bedtime story...word for word to her doll one day. It was for Josephine that he had made up his first *Just So Stories*.

Not until Kipling recovered from his own illness was he told of Josephine's death.

"I don't think it likely that I will ever come back to America," Kipling wrote after returning to England. "My little girl loved it dearly and it was in New York that we lost her."

Seven-year-old Josephine was forever his "lost child."

Leopards, Camels and Crabs

THE LEOPARD lived in a place called the High Veldt. It was there, as the Kipling story goes, that the "sclusivest sandiest-yellowish-brownest of all the catty-shaped kind of beasts got his spots."

The Veldt, or grassy plain, in "How the Leopard Got His Spots," is in Africa, where the Kiplings went by ship each winter. Unlike the unhappy winter crossing of the North Atlantic, which caused the death of little Josephine, the trips to South Africa were pleasant and especially enjoyable for Elsie and her brother. They loved the special attention they received from their father while on board ship.

Kipling on vacation was like a schoolboy freed from the schoolroom...ready to join a group of children for some fun. On the trips to South Africa he liked to gather all the youngest children on deck for storytelling

hour. Squatting down among a group of girls and boys, including his own, he would begin one of his stories: "In the days when everybody started fair, Best Beloved," he would recite in a deep sing-song voice…and continue with the story of "How the Camel Got His Hump" or "How the Rhinoceros Got His Skin."

Africa, its animals and setting were the source of many of the *Just So Stories*. None of them came directly from African folk tales although they were written in the same manner. They were Kipling's own inventions, except for "The Crab That Played with the Sea," which is taken from an authentic Malay tale. In the original tale, a giant crab sits over a large hole in the bottom of the sea. When the crab goes out for food, twice a day, the waters of the sea pour into the hole causing an ebb tide. When the crab returns to sit over the hole, the water remains at high tide.

In the folk tales of Asia and Africa, animals are given the power of gods. They can make the tides ebb, the rivers flow, the sun disappear, even carry mountains on their backs. Everything is possible….as it is in the *Just So Stories.*

It was Elsie who gave the stories their name, for like Josephine, she insisted that not a word be changed or a sentence left out. The stories, often repeated at bedtime, had to be told "just so" or she made her father go back and fill in the missing words.

WINTER TRIPS to Africa continued until Elsie and John were unable to be away from school for so many months. Family vacations were then taken closer to home. There were other trips during the year when Mr. and Mrs. Kipling traveled without the children. As one of Britain's well-known writers, Kipling was invited to give lectures and after-dinner speeches in many parts of Britain. And as the author of a great number of patriotic poems, Kipling received many honors and awards. Some he turned down, even one offered by the king and queen of England that would have made him a knight. Some he accepted, honorary awards given in very formal ceremonies.

With a good deal of amusement, he described one such event in a letter to his son:

"After arriving by train to Oxford University a man met me with my scarlet and grey gown. The gown looks rather like an African parrot." He was asked to wear it in a parade of scholars to be honored at the university. "We looked like boys at school," he told his son, "as we were lined up two-by-two."

"The men, dressed in long gowns of all colors, walked slowly down the High Street of Oxford. Just in front of me was Mark Twain who was also being honored," he said. "After entering an enormous room with marvelous windows, we were asked to sit on old oak benches to wait our turn. We waited — and waited — and waited. As each received his honors, we could hear the shouts and cheers in the distance. It was exactly like prisoners on a desert island hearing savages eating their companions."

The speeches and handshakes finished, Kipling was surprised and delighted to see "Uncle Crom," his old headmaster at Westward Ho there to congratulate him. It was "Crom" who first encouraged him to be a writer.

Several months later that same year, Kipling was on his way to Sweden to receive his greatest honor, the Nobel Prize in Literature. Kipling was only the seventh writer in the world to be given this award.

Alfred Nobel, a Swedish chemist and inventor, had left a large sum of money for this award. It is given for exceptional work in chemistry, physics, medicine, and international peace as well. This high honor is presented in a most formal ceremony by the king of Sweden. But in December of 1907, the king had just died.

The city of Stockholm was draped in black when the Kiplings arrived. Ceremonies were canceled or cut short. Kipling was given his gold medal and a hand-painted certificate in a quiet ceremony in the Town Hall and later invited to a banquet.

"They have eels in jelly and pickled herring and lobster and crabs and raw ham and dried salmon," wrote Kipling, "none of which Carrie let me eat. Isn't it a shame?" he complained in his letter to John and Elsie.

Stockholm was dark and mournful that winter. The Kiplings were happy to return to Sussex and their children.

"My Boy Jack"

ONCE AGAIN Kipling's fame made him the center of attention. He did not like it any better in England than he had in America. Their house, "The Elms" in Rottingdean, near the resort city of Brighton, attracted the curious and the tourists. The Kiplings looked for a house away from towns and tourists.

In a ride in his Locomobile through the Sussex countryside, Rudyard discovered the perfect house, "down a long rabbit-hole of a road," he said. It was miles from the railroad and from town. The sandstone building, with eleven chimneys, ample grounds and mill, was very old. The mill was even older. Much English history had occurred around Bateman's, as the house was called.

In the house were placed souvenirs of Kipling's past: a watercolor of Lake Rudyard, an Indian elephant god, two plaster plaques his father did for *The Jungle Books*. Kipling's writing table faced a row of windows looking out on the Sussex meadows. England was now his home. He no longer thought of living in America or in India or Africa. His thoughts turned to England's past, to the history his children had just begun to learn. Taking a piece of pale blue paper and his pen he began to write a story about the early history of Britain with Puck, a fairy-like being, as the guide to the past.

Puck of Pooks Hill made English history come alive. The hill in his story was just beyond the garden and history was in its very soil. Next came *Rewards and Fairies,* and *Below the Mill Dam,* books inspired by the countryside outside Kipling's window.

This large house in Sussex, though out of the way, was rarely empty of visitors while Elsie and John were growing up. There was a steady flow of relatives, old Sussex families, foreign guests, writers and children of all kinds. When his children left Bateman's to go to boarding school, the house seemed all too empty for Kipling.

"Dear Bird (Elsie)," wrote her father, "The house is four times emptier and five times larger than it was at eleven o'clock this morning."

The letter sent on the day she left for school in London tells about the ordinary details of his day and then continues: "There isn't any other news so I send you a few simple rules for Life in London." Rule one was about washing early and often with soap and hot water.

Rule two was not to roll on the grass, and rule three was never to eat penny buns, oysters, periwinkles or pepper-mints on the top of a bus. By rule seven, she was advised to avoid "pickled salmon, public meetings, crowded crossings...and overeating." The letter was signed "Daddo."

To John, who was ten and living in a boarding school in Rottingdean, he started his letters with the words, "Dear old Man," signing them "Dadda," "Your superiorly affectionate Dad," or "Your most loving Pater."

Kipling decorated his letters with amusing draw-ings, a habit since his own school days. Drawing gave him a special pleasure. The first edition of his *Just So Stories* included his pen and ink drawings of the dog-headed Baboon, a dijon, jaguars and armadillos. He spent many happy hours sketching, adding to his words the additional playfulness of his pictures.

In a letter written in June, 1909, Kipling included a sketch of John with many pairs of legs under his jacket; he said:..."Mother does nothing nowadays except knit. She knits when she walks in the garden or through the farms; she knits in the trains and when she rests in bed. I'm only glad she doesn't knit in her sleep. Her only explanation is that she is making stockings for you. When I sent you to school this term you had only two legs. How many more *have* you grown?"

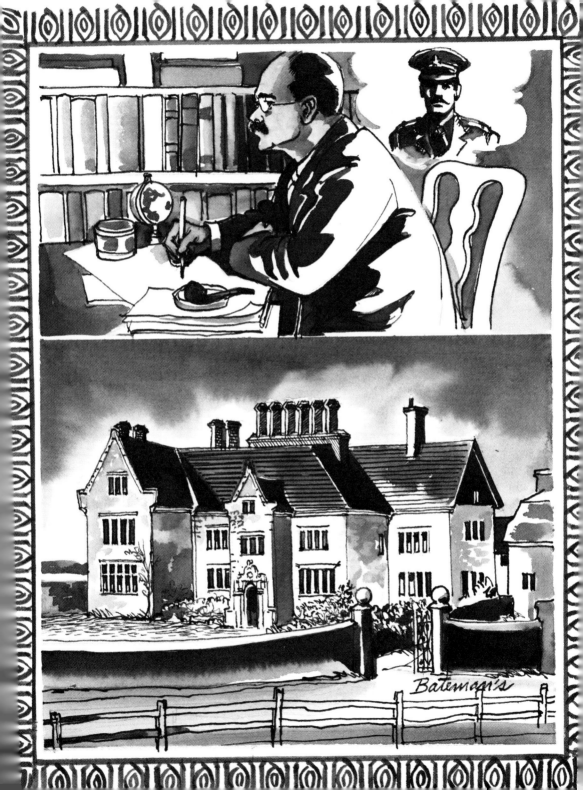

KIPLING wrote letters to his children to amuse them, to gently instruct them and to take away the pangs of homesickness. They were the same as a phone call from home at a time when there were no phones. The weather, their mother's health, visitors were mentioned and, on occasion, John's schoolwork was discussed. He was not a very good student and his brief letters home were often full of mistakes. It prompted his father to answer with some irritation in another letter:

HOWE WOOD YU LICK IT IF I ROTE YOU A LETER AL FUL OF MIS SPELD WURDS? I NO YU KNO KWITE WELL HOWE TO SPEL ONLI YU WONTE TAIK THE TRUBBLE TO THINCK?

"Your last letter is more vilely spelled than usual," his father said in despair. "Why *can't* you spell?"

VENICE, Paris, Cairo…from all parts of the globe, wherever Rudyard traveled, letters to his children were sent week by week, year by year. For Kipling, traveling had always been a way to relax, to find new material for his writing. Life at Bateman's remained the same, but the world Kipling saw on his trips was changing…and what he saw he did not like. In 1913, Europe seemed headed for war. It was the year John turned sixteen.

John was enrolled in Wellington College with plans to join the navy when he graduated. In 1914, the war Rudyard had anticipated broke out between France and Germany and Britain soon entered on the side of France. John was made an officer in the Irish Guards (the same as Kimball O'Hara's father in the book, *Kim)* and on his eighteenth birthday was shipped to France. Less than a week later, John was "missing in action." No trace of him was ever found. It is believed that he stepped on a land mine and was killed instantly. Kipling wrote this sad poem, *My Boy Jack,* in 1916:

> "Have you news of my boy Jack?"
> *Not this tide.*
> "When d'you think that he'll come back?"
> *Not with this wind blowing, and this tide.*
>
> "Has anyone else had word of him?"
> *Not this tide.*
> *For what is sunk will hardly swim,*
> *Not with this wind blowing, and this tide.*
>
> "Oh, dear, what comfort can I find?"
> *None this tide,*
> *Nor any tide, . . .*

Although Rudyard and Carrie were quite certain that their son was dead, they searched for news of him for years. This second tragedy destroyed Kipling's health. All the playfulness went out of his writing, and he only appeared in public when he considered it a necessity.

For many years Kipling continued to travel, to write, to see close friends, always returning to the quiet of Bateman's, his home for thirty-five years.

In January of 1936, while on the way to France for a winter holiday, Rudyard became ill and died. He was seventy-one. His ashes were placed in Westminster Abbey alongside those of England's most respected writers.

Bateman's has been left just as it was when he lived there. His books, his desk, his pen-wipes are standing as though ready to be used once the study empties of visitors. The large woven wastebasket seems to await the crumpled blue papers with words crossed out, corrected and recorrected…until, at last, a story unfolded…

This, O Best Beloved, is a story — a new and a wonderful story — a story quite different from the other stories — a story about the Most Wise Sovereign Sulieman-bin-Daoud…

…a story "just so."

GLOSSARY

ayah — Indian name for nursemaid

burra sahib bahadur — A big, brave gentleman

dhow — a sailing vessel

ghee — clarified butter

griffin — an imaginary animal of the Middle Ages

pugdog — a type of small bulldog

rickshaw — a light, two-wheeled carriage pulled by one, or two or three men that was common in parts of the Far East

rupees — Indian money

sahib — "Lord" title applied to any gentleman and most Europeans

veldt — a grassy plain in Africa

wombats — a mammal of Australia resembling a small bear

BIBLIOGRAPHY

Amis, Kingsley. *Rudyard Kipling and His World*. Thames & Hudson, 1975.

Birkenhead, Lord Fredrick W. *Kipling*. Random House, 1978.

Carrington, Charles. *Rudyard Kipling: His Life and Work*. Macmillan, 1955.

Gilbert, Elliot L. *Rudyard Kipling, O Beloved Kids*. Harcourt, Brace, Jovanovich, 1983.

Green, Roger L. *Kipling and the Children*. Elek Brooks, Ltd., 1965.

Kipling, Rudyard. *Something of Myself: For My Friends Known and Unknown*. Doubleday, 1937.

Otto, Margaret. *Mr. Kipling's Elephant*. Knopf, 1961.

Stefanson, V. *Kipling and Vermont*.

Stewart, J. I. M. *Rudyard Kipling*. Dodd, Mead & Co., 1966.

Wilson, Angus. *The Strange Ride of Rudyard Kipling*. Viking, 1977.

MONOGRAPHS:

Rodd, Lewis. *Ruddy, The Black Sheep*.

Sutcliff, Rosemary. *Rudyard Kipling*. Bodley Head, 1960.